Donated by

The Case of the Kidnapped Collie

The Case of the Kidnapped Collie

John R. Erickson

Illustrations by Gerald L. Holmes

Viking

VIKING
Published by the Penguin Group
Penguin Putnam Books for Young Readers, 345 Hudson Street, New York, New York 10014, U.S.A.
Penguin Books Ltd, 27 Wrights Lane, London W8 5TZ, England
Penguin Books Australia Ltd, Ringwood, Victoria, Australia
Penguin Books Canada Ltd, 10 Alcorn Avenue, Toronto, Ontario, Canada M4V 3B2
Penguin Books (N.Z.) Ltd, 182-190 Wairau Road, Auckland 10, New Zealand

Penguin Books Ltd, Registered Offices: Harmondsworth, Middlesex, England

First published in the United States of America
by Maverick Books, Gulf Publishing Company, 1996
Published by Puffin Books, a division of Penguin Putnam Books for Young Readers, 1999
Published by Viking, a division of Penguin Putnam Books for Young Readers, 2000

1 3 5 7 9 10 8 6 4 2

ISBN 0-670-88433-2

Printed in the United States of America
Set in New Century Schoolbook

To Mary Kate Tripp, book editor
for the Amarillo News-Globe, *who has done*
more to encourage reading and writing
in the Texas Panhandle than anyone I know.
Thanks, MKT.

CONTENTS

Sorry, But I Can't Reveal the Collie's Name

It's me again, Hank the Cowdog. As you might have noticed, this story is called *The Case of the Kidnapped Collie.* Pretty spooky, huh? You bet it is.

In fact, it's so spooky that I can't reveal the collie's name. It might give the kids too much of a scare. See, I happen to know that this certain unnamed collie is popular with the kids, and if they knew she was going to get captured by a ferocious cannibal . . .

Oops, I didn't want to mention that either, the cannibal part. Forget I said it. Let's just say that I was misquoted. I was discussing camels and you thought I said "cannibals," but I didn't.

I said nothing, almost nothing at all, about collies or cannibals, and now we can get on with the story.

Have we discussed bird dogs lately? Maybe not, and maybe we should. I don't like 'em, never have, and the main reason I don't like 'em is that I've known a few . . . well, one anyway . . . and I didn't like him, not even a little bit.

Remember Plato, the stupid, spotted, stick-tailed, dumb-bunny bird dog? You might recall that Plato was . . . I don't know what.

How can you describe a guy who shows up at the very exact moment when your fondesh wist is never to see him again? Fondest wish, I should say. At the very exact moment when it appears that you will finally get to spend a few precious moments with the woman of your dreams, there he is—the bird dog.

He shows up like flies at a picnic—unwanted, uncalled for, totally irrelevant to the situation.

Always grinning. Always the perfect gentleman. So kind and friendly it makes you ill, but what *really* makes you ill is that you want so badly to beat him up.

But who can beat up a guy who's always nice? That's the problem with Plato. He's too dumb to know how much everybody hates him, and he's too nice to be told in the usual manner—a thrashing.

So he ends up winning the heart of my girlfriend, and I end up wondering how dumb he can be when he wins all the time. And the more I think about it, the madder I get, and excuse me for a moment while I bang my head against this tree over here.

BONK! BONK! BONK!

That's better. Where were we? Oh yes, trees.

Trees are large plants. Their roots grow downward while their branches grow upward toward the sky. Nobody knows why they do it that way, but the important thing about trees is that you should never bang your head against one.

Their bark is worse than their bite, you might say.

A little humor there. Trees don't actually bark, see, but they have this hard layer of . . . maybe you got it.

Okay. All trees should be equipped with a sign that says, "Don't bang your head on this thing, no matter how much you hate bird dogs, because it will mess you up and the tree will never feel a thing."

But the point is that I had no use for bird dogs and had no reason for ever wanting to see one again. But I did.

It all began . . . hmmm, when did it begin? Was it in the summer? No. Winter? No. Spring? Don't think so. Then that leaves . . .

. . . the leaves were turning yellow. Okay, here we go. It was in the fall of the year, of course it was, you ninny, because that's when bird season starts, and it follows from simple logic that you begin seeing bird dogs around the start of bird season.

Sorry, I shouldn't have called you a ninny. That was uncalled for. You did your best and you can't help it that your memory moves quite a bit slower than . . . well, mine, you might say. Mine operates at fifty megahurts and it hurts pretty mega right now after banging my head against the stupid . . .

I've got a headache and I shouldn't have called you a ninny.

Anyways, it all began in the spring of the year, toward the end of November, as I recall. Yes, it's all coming back now. We'd had several cold fronts and the mornings were cool and crisp. The chinaberries had shed most of their leaves and the days were getting shorter.

And on one of those lovely autumn afternoons, I happened to overhear a conversation between Slim and Loper, the two cowboys on this outfit.

Or let's put it this way. They think of themselves as cowboys and they take pride in their cowboy skills, but on this particular afternoon they found themselves involved in some serious non-cowboy work.

They were doing some reconstruction work on the feed barn, see, and they had reported to the job site in their carpenter costumes. Instead of the usual cowboy boots and hats, they showed up in caps, overalls, and lace-up boots.

Instead of arming themselves with ropes and spurs, as usual, they had brought hammers and saws and pry bars. They had even brought a device that I had thought was against the law on our outfit: a tape measure.

No kidding, Slim and Loper had actually brought a tape measure to the job site! I was dumb-foundered. I mean, after years and years of wood-butchery and the very worst displays of cowboy carpentry, why had they suddenly decided to measure their boards?

I couldn't understand it. Maybe Loper had read an article on woodworking and had run into a reference to something called a "tape measure." It must have given him such a jolt that he decided to buy one at the lumberyard and try it out.

Slim set the tone for the project when he pulled out a foot of tape and squinted at it for a long time.

"Say, do these little marks between the inch lines mean anything?"

To which Loper replied, "Those are for brain surgeons."

"Good. I can't hardly see 'em."

And away they went, hacking and sawing and pounding. Would you care to listen in on one of their high-tech conversations? Okay, they had just sawed two boards and were putting them in place.

Loper: "Do they fit?"

Slim: "Nope."

Loper: "Are they close?"

Slim: "Nope."

Loper: "Do they touch?"

Slim: "Yep, barely."

Loper: "Nail 'em. We ain't building pianos."

I don't mean to scoff or make fun of their pathetic efforts, but if you think I'm exaggerating, just take a tour of the feed barn sometime and pay close attention to the west side.

Anyways, it was November and I had noticed the many signs of fall. The locust and chinaberry trees had . . . I've already mentioned that, but I didn't say anything about the cockleburs.

You know for sure that fall has arrived when all the horses on the ranch start wearing cockleburs in their tails, manes, and . . . whatever you call that bunch of hair on their foreheads . . . bangs, forelocks, padlocks . . . I'm sorry I brought it up.

The horses get involved with cockleburs, is the point, and even we dogs collect a few of them. In the fall of the year, it's almost impossible to conduct ranch business without picking up some cockleburs.

Other signs of fall: The hawks and kites have left and other types of birds have moved in, such as your crows, your bluebirds, your robins, and your sandhill cranes.

And wild turkeys, but we'll get to that later on.

Oh yes, and the wasps. All at once, they were everywhere and they were lazy and it didn't take much talent to get stung by one, the hateful little things.

Oh, and one last symptom of fall in our country is that you begin seeing tarantula spiders. You never see them until the fall of the year (which is sure okay with me), then all at once you see them crossing the road.

Me, I can get along just fine without tarantulas. They are big and hairy-legged and ugly, and let's change the subject. They give me the creeps.

Where were we? Oh yes, the Board Butchers were trying to repair the west side of the feed barn. Around two o'clock, they stopped and took a break. And it was then that I heard the bad news.

I happened to be seated nearby, beaming glares at Pete the Barncat and trying to extract three cocklebburs from my coat of hair. I had been ignoring most of Slim and Loper's conversation, since it had been fairly boring, but I perked up when I realized that they were discussing a dog.

"You know, Slim, I've never gotten much of a

kick out of hunting quail, and just the other day I realized why."

"'Cause you're a terrible shot?"

"No. The sport in bird hunting, the real sport, comes from watching the dogs work, and I'm talking about good dogs, trained dogs, dogs that are born and bred for birds."

"Yalp, but instead of owning a bird dog, you've got one that's bird-brained."

The conversation stopped and I realized that they were both staring at . . . well, ME, you might say. I thumped my tail on the ground and gave them my most sincere cowdog smile.

Slim: "See what I mean? He's eatin' cockleburs."

What? Was he trying to be funny? All right, maybe I did have a cocklebur in my mouth at that very moment, but I was extracting it from my coat, thank you, and not EATING it.

And just to prove it, to show what a silly mockery he was making of my dignity, I spit it out. There!

I wasn't eating cockleburs.

Nor was I amused by his childish remark about . . . what was it? Something about a "bird-brained dog"?

Not funny, not funny at all, but of course he laughed at his own stale joke.

He thought he was such a comedian.

Loper continued. "Anyhow, I invited Billy to come over this afternoon and bring that dog of his. I guess he's a pretty good quail dog."

HUH?

My head shot up and so did my ears.

Billy? Quail dog? Holy smokes, Billy was our neighbor down the creek and his so-called quail dog was named . . .

You guessed it. Plato.

A Porkchop on the Eighth Floor

My eyes locked on Loper's face. He wasn't kidding. He had actually invited . . . oh brother, that's all I needed: My least favorite bird dog in the whole world would soon be invading my ranch and my privacy!

I was outraged, and just to show how angry I felt about this, I turned a Poisoned Glare on him. It should have ruined his day and made him feel guilty about his careless decision, but it didn't. He didn't even notice.

Instead, he pushed himself up and said, "We'd better get this mess finished. Billy said he'd be here around four."

Moments later, the air was filled with the sounds of their work—crashing and banging. It hurt my ears so I decided to move my business to a quieter location.

Also, my feelings were hurt. Apparently it had never occurred to the Ranch Executives (I'll not mention any names) to give ME a shot at the bird dog job.

Can you believe that? I couldn't. I was amazed.

Shocked.

Deeply hurt.

Wounded almost beyond repair.

I mean, what's the big deal about pointing birds? Ask the best dog trainers. Ask an experienced hunter. Ask, well, ME, since I'm here and handy and happen to have some pretty strong opinions on this matter.

What's the big deal about pointing birds? IT'S NO BIG DEAL AT ALL. Any dog with half a brain could point a bunch of stupid twittering birds. Drover could be a bird dog. Pete the Barncat could be a bird dog, only he's not a dog, so . . .

Well, you get the drift. It was totally ridiculous that Loper would even consider bringing in an outsider from the outside, when he already had a dog on staff that could do . . . well, almost anything short of magic tricks and miracles, and sure as thunder wouldn't have any trouble pointing quail.

Sorry. I'm getting carried away. My anger is showing. I tried to pretend that I didn't care, that my feelings weren't involved in . . .

I had thought we were friends, pals, companions, comrades, and then he . . . oh well.

They would be sorry, yes they would, all the scoffers and laughers and scaffers and those of little faith. They would eat crowbars before this thing was finished.

Anyway, I had better things to do with my time. I marched right over to Pete. "What are you grinning about, Kitty?"

I didn't wait to hear his answer. I wasn't interested in his answer. I barked in his face and ran him up the nearest tree. It served him right. And he needed the exercise. I'd noticed that he was getting fat.

And besides, chasing him up a tree made me feel much better.

I left the Wood Butchers, hiked over to the gas tanks, and flopped down on my gunnysack. Drover was already there—had been there most of the day, in fact, sleeping his life away.

It was a warm, rather lazy afternoon, and it wasn't long until I began to notice that my eyelids were . . . snork murk . . . exhausted from the rigor mortis of protecting the . . . skonk snirk . . .

Okay, maybe I dozed off, but I deserved a rest. I had just pulled three shifts in a row and had put in, oh, eighteen or twenty hours straight—and we're talking no breaks, no sleep, no nothing but rigors and exhausting work.

I was totally wiped out. Otherwise, I wouldn't have fallen asnork in the middle of the afternork.

Drover was making his usual orchestra of noises: grunting, wheezing, yipping. He's the noisiest sleeper I ever met. Oh, and he also quivers and jerks in his sleep, and sometimes his eyelids fall open and you can see his eyeballs rolling around.

I didn't happen to be looking at his eyeballs because I was deeply involved in a delicious dream about . . . mercy! The lovely Miss Beulah, girl of my dreams, woman of my life, the world's most gorgeous . . .

I almost said "collie gal," but our use of the word "collie" is still under tight security, don't you see, and I didn't say it. Sorry.

Where were we? Oh yes. Pete came along just then and ruined my dream by slapping my tail with his paw.

Why does he do such things? Well, he's a cat and cats get some kind of twisted pleasure out of tormenting things, such as birds, lizards, mice, and dog tails.

I knew he was there but tried to ignore him, hoping he might go away. You see, I knew that if I gave him my full attention, I would have to give up my dreams of Beulah and I wasn't ready for that.

Hence, when he slapped at my tail, I moved it ever so slightly to the south. Did that stop him? Did he take a hint? Did he care that the Head of Ranch Security was trying to recharge his precious bodily fluids and get ready for another drooling night on Life's Front Lines?

Grueling, I should say.

Oh no. Since my tail had moved, that proved that it was attached to some living object that he could torment, which made him want to slap it again.

So he slapped it again, a little harder this time, and I moved it again, with a bit more vigor, and I'm sure that made his sneaky little cat eyes grow wide with delight—although I couldn't see them because mine were closed.

And he slapped it again, only this time he introduced claws into the equation. How foolish of him. I can be broadminded about a cat who slaps my tail around with his paws, but add claws and it changes the deal entirely.

Do you know why? BECAUSE IT HURTS,

that's why. My tail is a very sensitive piece of equipment. It's not a brick or a tree root or a piece of windmill pipe. If you prick it, it will bleed. If you stab it, it will hurt. If you step on it, it will bring forth yelps of pain and sorrow.

Hencely, as the sharp little impulses of pain began pouring into Data Control, my eyelids began to quiver and a ferocious growl began to rumble in the deep recessitudes of my throat.

My head came up. My ears shot up to Full Alert Position. Okay, one of them did while the other went sideways into the Huh? Position.

My eyes sprang open and I saw . . . not much, actually, just a large blur. It's the sort of image we get when our scanning devices are focused at conflicting angles. In the Security Business, we sometimes refer to this as Temporary Eye-Crosserosis.

It usually occurs when a dog comes roaring out of a deep sleep, opens his eyes, and tries to figure out whether it's raining or Tuesday.

I know this is pretty heavy technical stuff, but it will give you a little glimpse at how life is lived on the other side of the Veil of Secrecy. Over there, where we live, life is always real but never real simple.

Where was I? Oh yes, the tree. I had just banged my head against . . . forget the tree. I had come roaring out of a deep dark sleep and just for a brief instant my eyes were crossed and my brain was in Scrambled Mode, but that lasted only the briefest of instants.

And suddenly I exclaimed, "Purple hominy regardless of feathered turnip greens and darkest porkchop!"

Then an image came into focus: the face of a cat, the face of a grinning cat who was smirking. The pieces of the puzzle began falling into place and suddenly I exclaimed, "Is this the eighth floor?"

The image of the alleged cat shook his head,

and then he said in a whiny voice, "Hi, Hankie. Were you sleeping on the job?"

At that very moment, Data Control kicked in at full blast and I received a very important transmission: It was neither raining nor Tuesday. It was Pete the Barncat.

I glared at the little snipe with eyes of purest steel.

"Okay, Kitty, let's get right to the point. We've just learned that there's a porkchop on the eighth floor, and don't bother denying it. We've followed the trail of turnip greens and it leads . . ."

I cut my eyes from side to side. All at once what I was saying didn't make a great deal of sense. I shot a glance back to the cat. Had he noticed? I had to find out how much he knew.

"Pete, do you know anything about this porkchop deal?"

He grinned and shook his head. "No, I don't, Hankie, but I would just love to hear about it. Tell me about the porkchop on the eighth floor."

I marched a few steps away and took a deep breath of . . . well, air, of course. What else would . . . anyway, it seemed to clear my head.

"I'm sorry, Pete, but I'm not at liberty to discuss a case in progress. Our files are not open to the public, and they're especially not open to public cats."

"Mmmmmm! It must have been very secret."

"Exactly. It was so secret, in fact, that if I revealed even one particle of information, I would have to arrest you for being in possession of Dangerous Particles of Information."

"Oooooooo! My goodness, Hankie, how do you carry all that dangerous information around in your head?"

I could see that he was impressed. He should have been. Maybe he wasn't as dumb as I had thought. I marched back over to where he was sitting.

"That's a good question, Kitty. Unfortunately, I'm not at liberty to say any more about our techniques for gathering and storing intelligence data. Sorry."

"Oh darn." He stared at me with those weird yellowish eyes with the little slit down the middle. "I was so eager to learn more about the porkchop on the eighth floor."

"What are you talking about?"

"Well, Hankie, that's what you said when you," he grinned, "woke up from your nap during working hours."

Perhaps you're thinking that all of this sounds slightly ridiculous, but it's leading up to something very important. You see, in the course of the conversation, Pete revealed . . . well, you'll find out soon enough.

It had to do with a robbery that was taking place on my ranch in broad daylight, and that's all I can tell you.

My Clever Interrogation of the Cat

I felt the hair rising on the back of my neck. "Number One, I wasn't asleep. Number Two, I never said anything about a so-called porkchop on the so-called ninth floor."

"Eighth floor, Hankie."

"Don't try to put words into my mouth, cat. I know what I said."

"I thought you didn't say it."

"I didn't say it, and that's my whole point. I didn't say it because it was totally ridiculous. There is no porkchop and there is no eighth floor, but I know what you're doing."

"Oh really?"

"Yes." I stuck my nose in his face. "You're trying to send up a smoke screen of meaningless words to conceal the fact that you stuck your claws into my tail. Don't try to deny it."

"All right, Hankie, I won't."

"Huh? Well, I . . . I'm shocked, Pete. I don't know what to say. I was sure you'd deny it and then try to draw me into an argument."

He blinked his eyes and grinned. Why was he always grinning? It made me uneasy.

"Oh no, Hankie. I used to do things like that but then I learned my lesson."

"Oh? What lesson are we talking about?"

He licked his left paw before speaking. I studied and memorized his every move, just in case this was another of his famous frauds.

"I learned that it's almost impossible to fool the Head of Ranch Security."

"Well! Imagine that. I can hardly believe my ears. In fact, I don't believe my ears. Say it again."

"All right, Hankie, whatever you wish. I've learned that I can't fool you and that's why I admit that I stuck my little claws into the end of your tail."

I paced off to the east. My mind was trying to absorb this astonishing piece of news and it needed a moment to catch up.

"You've come a long way, Pete, and to be real honest about it, we never thought you'd change. Our profiles and projections showed you in the Normal Range of cats: sneaky, hateful, untrustworthy, treacherous, and, well, not real smart, if I may be so blunt."

"Oh, go right ahead, Hankie. I realize that I'm only a cat."

"That's true, Pete, and you can't help it that cats are . . . how can I say this?"

"Dumb?"

"Good word, Pete, great word. I wouldn't have

thought of putting it that way but, yes, 'dumb' sort of captures the overall . . ."

"Condition, Hankie?"

"Yes, right, exactly. The overall condition of catness." I marched over and gave the little guy a pat on the back. "Hey Pete, I feel we've reached a breakthrough situation. I mean, all these years we've been enemies and now, all at once, you admit that you're stupid and . . . hey, we've got nothing left to fight about!"

He purred and continued to grin, only now it didn't bother me because I realized that he was being sincere.

"At last we're at peace, Hankie."

"Right, and it wasn't so bad was it? Did you ever dream that making peace would be so easy?"

"Never did, Hankie. Oh, is Beulah coming?"

I glared at him. "What did you just say?"

"I wondered if Beulah would be coming with Plato."

I cut my eyes from side to side. "I hadn't thought of that, Pete, so how did you happen to think of it?"

"Oh, I heard the cowboys say that Plato was coming. Every time Plato comes around, Beulah is with him. I just wondered."

I marched a few steps away. My mind was

racing. "Go on, Pete. I have a feeling that this is leading somewhere."

"Well . . . if she comes to watch her bird dog boyfriend perform, I thought it might be nice if you . . ."

He was staring at me with those weird full-moon eyes. And grinning. And flicking the end of his tail back and forth.

"If I what? What kind of sneaky tricks are running through that sneaky little mind of yours?"

"Oh, you might not be interested, Hankie."

I stomped over to him and stuck my nose in his face. "I'm not interested, Kitty, but part of my job on this ranch is to stay one step ahead of the cats. Out with it."

He drew circles in the dust with his paw. "Well, if I were you, I'd want to impress Miss Beulah."

"Ha! Me impress Miss Beulah? Hey Pete, for your information, she's crazy about me and . . . impress her in what way? I mean, just for laughs I want to hear the rest of this."

He blinked his eyelids and grinned. "Well, Hankie, you can show her and everyone else that you can hunt birds as well as Plato. I know a way."

I almost took the bait. I almost asked him to tell me more, but caught myself just in time. Chuckling, I turned and walked a few steps away.

"Ha, ha, ha. Pete, you're the champ when it

comes to scheming, but there are a couple of holes in your ointment. Number one, Beulah probably won't come. Number two, if she does come, I plan to be very busy with my routine work. Number three, Plato is just a minor irritation to me. Number four, I don't need to impress him or Beulah or anyone else. That would be childish and silly.

"Number five, I have no interest in birds. Zero. Zilch. Birds are totally boring. And number six, this conversation is over. Now run along and catch a mouse."

He started to leave in that sliding gliding walk of his. "Whatever you think, Hankie, but if you change your mind, I'll be around."

"Fine. Great. I won't change my mind. Thanks for trying to be helpful, but I don't need any help. Good-bye."

He left. Peace at last. What a crazy idea, me trying to impress Beulah with . . . actually, it wasn't such a . . . but on the other hand, I didn't need to impress her—her or anyone else.

Hey, I was comfortable just being who I was: Head of Ranch Security, owner of a huge ranch and many cattle; a heroic guard dog, a fairly handsome feller; winner of countless awards and also unusually handsome and charming.

Wasn't that enough? Was there more? I didn't

think so. If Beulah couldn't admire who I was, the real Hank the Cowdog; if she needed circus acts and magic tricks, then . . .

I found my eyes following the cat. He was slinking along with his tail stuck straight up in the air, rubbing on every tree and past he posted. Post he passed. And every now and then, I noticed that he was tossing lazy glances back at me.

Hmmmm. Was it possible that he knew something that . . . no. Simple logic told me that anything known to a cat would be known first to a dog. Therefore . . .

Therefore the little sneak certainly looked as though he knew something important, and the best cure for that false impression was for me to stop looking at him.

Some cats need more ignoring than others. Pete requires a lot. And so it was that I embarked on a new policy of Total Ignoration of the Cat, which turned out to be pretty easy because at that very moment my ears picked up the tiny microwaves of an Incoming Vehicle.

The big question that loomed before me then was, AUTHORIZED VEHICLE OR TRESPASSER?

I did a Direct Downlink Feed to Data Control and got a flashing message on the huge screen of my mind: TRESPASSER!

Well, you know me. There are several things I don't allow on my ranch and one of them is trespassers and unauthorized intrusions.

Okay, that's two things but they mean about the same thing and neither one was allowed. That pickup had no business on our outfit and it was fixing to get the whole nine yards of barking and threatening gestures.

"Drover, we have a very important mission ahead of us and we're fixing to go to Red Alert. Are you ready for some combat?"

He leaped to his feet and began staggering around in circles. His eyes were crooked, his ears were crooked. It appeared to me that his mind might also be crooked.

"Is it my turn to bat?"

"I didn't say anything about batting, Drover, and Life is not a mere game."

"Oh my gosh, then who's on first?"

"You're still asleep, son. Look at me and tell me how many fingers I'm holding up."

He turned his eyes in my direction. They were still crooked. "Thirty-seven?"

"Wrong. Dogs don't have fingers. Therefore, the correct answer is zero."

"Zero! No wonder I'm so cold. Water freezes at thirty-two."

"Yes, but you said thirty-seven, so you're wrong again."

He blinked his eyes and looked around. "Where am I? What are we talking about?"

"We're in our bedroom under the gas tanks. You've been sleeping your life away and I just asked if you were ready for some combat."

"Not really."

"What?"

"I said, 'Combat. Oh boy.'"

"That's the spirit. We'll go to Full Flames on all engines and regroup in front of the house, and don't get lost."

"Well, I hope this old leg . . ."

I didn't wait around to hear about his "old leg." I had heard it all before, not once or twice but ten thousand times, enough that I was beginning to suspect that he was a hypocardiac.

Anyways, I didn't have time to hang around and listen to him whine about his leg. I went to Full Flames and roared around the south side of the house, and sure enough, looming up before my very eyes was an unauthorized vehicle.

The Unwelcome Guest Arrives

It was a reddish-colored Chevy pickup. Reddish but not exactly red. Macaroon. Macaroni. Maroni.

What do you call that color that is almost red but not quite? Or to put it another way, who cares? It was a reddish Chevy pickup and it had no business on my ranch and . . .

Maroon. There we go. It was a maroon-colored Chevy pickup, and it had no business driving on my ranch.

Right away, I went to Bark the Alarm and Alert the House. I knew Sally May would be . . . a bird dog in the back? Holy smokes, it appeared that I had just intercepted a shipment of illegal bird dogs, right there on my ranch! This case promised to be more . . .

Huh? The alleged bird dog spoke. Waved a paw. Smiled a big sloppy smile.

"Hank, by golly, it's great to see you again! Just great. How's the ranch? I hear we're going to hunt some birds, huh? Great. Hope you can come along."

I, uh, cancelled the Red Alert. It appeared that we had jumped to hasty conclusions about the . . . uh . . . the shipment of illegal . . .

It was Billy's pickup, and there for a moment I had . . . he had traded pickups since I'd seen him and . . . no big deal, is the point. Billy was always welcome on our ranch, even though he was hauling a bird dog who had been invited by other parties and I had no control over that.

I cancelled Alert the House and gave Drover the order to shift into Escort Formation. We did the shift in the twinkling of an eyeball. Drover took right flank and I took left, and we gave Billy a safe escort all the way down to the corrals.

The moment he came to a stop, I rushed to the pickup and applied the Ranch Trademark to all four tires, and we're talking about lightning speed. I blasted 'em, fellers, just knocked the centers right out of those four tires.

Have you ever wondered why we do that, why it's such an important job for the Head of Ranch Security?

I'm not sure I should reveal it. It's pretty secret. Very secret, in fact, so secret that even some dogs don't know the reason behind it.

Do I dare go public with this information? Better not. Hey, if it fell into the wrong hands . . . oh well, maybe it won't hurt. But just to be on the safe side, don't blab it around.

Okay, here it is, the whole truth behind the Marking Tires Procedure. That procedure places a special secret CHEMICAL LOCK on all four tires which totally immobilizes the vehicle.

No kidding. It can't be driven away until we supply the proper codes which unlock the chemical so-forth.

And if we don't happen to supply the secret codes, the vehicle becomes totally worthless. I mean, they have to send out a wrecker from town and tow the thing off the ranch. It's that powerful.

Pretty impressive, huh? You bet it is and now you know the whole story, but don't blab it around because . . . well, just think about it. If word of this ever got out to the general public, nobody from town would ever come out to visit Loper and Sally May.

They'd get lonely and lose all their friends. I mean, people would be afraid to risk it. Those cars and pickups are expensive.

Actually, we very seldom go to the extreme of Total Lockdown. Most of our cases turn out to be routine. We apply the Chemical Lock, check out the drivers, supply the codes, and turn 'em loose.

The last thing we need on the ranch is a bunch of abandoned cars and pickups. The place would start looking like a junkyard.

No, we usually turn 'em loose—but when we turn 'em loose, they're marked with Invisible Electroloids, which means that we can run a tracer on them any time we choose.

You never realized all this was going on, did you? You probably thought we dogs were just . . . I don't know, going through some foolish ritual, I suppose. Ha! Foolish to those who don't understand, maybe, but to those of us in Security Work, it's all part of a very clever master plan.

I'm sorry but that's all I can reveal at this moment, and I hope I haven't revealed too much. There's some danger in . . . I've already said that.

Now, where were we? Let's see . . .

Ah yes, we had just given the pickup Safe Escort down to the corrals and had marked all four tires, virtually immobilizing the macaroon-colored pickup. Once I had applied the Chemical Lockdown Agent, that pickup didn't move an inch.

At that point, I eased over to the vicinity of the pickup door and began a Snifferation of Billy's pant legs. This is another standard procedure we follow every time new people come onto the ranch. Even though I knew Billy, I had to check him out.

Sniff, sniff.

Hmmm, very interesting, very interesting indeed. The tiny pieces of the puzzle began . . .

Actually, I couldn't make much sense out of it. His pant legs smelled exactly like blue jean material, which sort of fit the overall pattern since he was wearing . . . well, blue jeans, you might say.

Not much there, but I pressed on with the Snifferation, just in case he . . . BONK! . . . just in case he suddenly kicked me on the nose with his boot heel and said, "Get away, bozo." Which is what he did, and yes, it did hurt, but at least I had gotten . . .

At least I had gotten my nose damaged and I suddenly lost my desire to sniff out his stupid . . .

Drover had just arrived on the scene—late, as always, huffing and puffing, as always, and limping.

"Drover, I've got a little job for you. Sniff out Billy's pant legs and give me a full report."

"Well . . ."

"That's a direct order. We don't have a moment to spare."

"There's one in the back of his pickup."

Our eyes met. "What?"

"I said, there's a spare in the back of his pickup."

"That's a bird dog."

"No, it's a spare tire. I saw it myself."

I went nose to nose with the runt and showed him some fangs. "Oh yeah? Well, I'm tired of arguing with you, so spare me the details."

"Gosh, that was good: tired and spare, like a spare tire."

I found myself sharing a little chuckle with him. "It was pretty good, wasn't it?"

"Yeah, it was great. Did you think it up yourself?"

"Oh yeah, sure. It was no big deal. It just popped out of my mouth, as a matter of fact."

"Boy, I wish I could do things like that. I never can remember a joke, and then when I do, I forget."

"Actually, Drover, it was more of a pun than a joke, a clever play on words."

"I ate a crayon once. Made me sick."

"Yes, but I said 'play on,' not crayon."

"Oh. Well, I never ate a playon."

"No, I suppose . . . uh . . . not." I blinked my eyes

and gave my head a shake. "Drover, were we talking about something?"

"No, I don't think so. We were just standing here, telling jokes."

"I see. Yes, of course."

I moved away from him. All at once I felt that my thought processes had turned to mush. This had occurred to me before, and it always seemed to happen when I was standing close to Drover. There was something about the little mutt . . . oh well.

I turned my attention to other matters.

Plato had jumped out of the pickup and was running around with his nose to the ground. I saw no great harm in being cordial to him. I mean, he HAD been invited to our ranch and, what the heck, he wasn't such a bad guy.

See, I could get along with Plato, when it was just him and me. Our problems in getting along had always been related to Beulah. Beulah wasn't around so we had nothing to fight about.

We had nothing about which to fight. About. Which.

You should never use a preposition to end a sentence with, but who cares about prepositions? Not me. I'm a very busy dog, and besides, a Head of Ranch Security can end a sentence any way he wants.

The point is, I could tolerate Plato by himself, and being cordial to him once in a while wouldn't kill me. In fact, there's a wise old saying about . . . something . . . being kind to others who are inferior and I can't remember it, but it's a great wise old saying.

Anyways, Plato had his nose to the ground and was streaking around in front of the corrals. Have you ever watched a bird dog going through this kind of routine?

I don't mean to scoff or make fun, but he looked totally ridiculous and absurd. I mean, here was a dog who was running around like a . . . I don't know, a Stealth Bomber, I suppose, with his neck thrust out and his nose to the ground and his tail thrown out behind like a fishing rod.

And he was SO SERIOUS about acting SO SILLY that I didn't know whether to laugh or feel sorry for him. See, what made it so ridiculous was that he was looking for quail, and I happened to know that there wasn't a quail within two miles of our present location.

Our quail stayed in the sand draws and up in the canyons. I knew that for a fact because . . . well, without revealing too much about my business affairs, I can tell you that our Security Division monitored the location and movements of *every covey of quail on the ranch.*

We knew them, knew their positions, their habitabits, their trails, their feeding grounds, their nesting grounds, the whole nine yards.

And there was poor old Plato, being a totally sincere vacuum sweeper and searching for birds that weren't there. Or even close.

No, it wouldn't hurt me to be kind to such a dumbbell.

The Angelic Kangaroo

He came bounding up to where I was standing. "Great day, huh Hank? I just live for the first day of bird season and by golly here it is."

"Yes, it's here. Bird season."

"As you probably know, Hank, I spend all year working out and getting ready for this."

"I didn't know that."

"Oh yes, I work out every day, every single day. I jog, I swim, retrieve sticks, point tennis shoes. I even do breathing exercises, Hank, to keep my nose in shape. The nose is SO important, Hank, so important."

"Yeah, if a guy didn't have one, he'd look a little strange."

He stared at me for a long moment. "Okay,

you're joking, right? Ha, ha. That was good. By the first day of bird season, I'm so excited that . . . well, just look at me, Hank. I'm shivering. Is that being excited or what?"

Sure enough, he was shivering all over. "That's being excited."

"But I feel I'm in shape, Hank, maybe the best shape of my life. You may remember that last season I pulled a muscle in my shoulder."

"I guess I missed that."

"Did you? I got a bad muscle pull on opening day, and Hank, I'll be honest with you. I thought my career was over. It was that bad."

"Hmmm. I'll be derned."

"Right. But I worked through it, Hank. I went into a different program and made it back for the third week of the season."

"Wow."

"Thanks, Hank. It was tense and I had some trouble with depression, but," he gave me a wink, "everything works out, doesn't it?"

"How's Beulah?"

"Excuse me? Oh, Beulah. Beulah is . . ." He smiled, closed his eyes, opened them again, and looked up at the sky. "Beulah is . . . how can I find words to, to express the Beulah-ness of Beulah?"

"I don't know."

"I often say, Hank, that Beulah is a painting in fur, a work of sculpture that lives and breathes before our very eyes. Now, if you'll excuse me, I'd better finish my warm-ups. Will you be hunting with us?"

"Oh sure, you bet. I know a couple of things about birds myself."

"Do you? Great. I didn't know you were into birds. You've been practicing, I guess, working out, getting all prepared for the big day, huh?"

"Oh yes."

"Great! We'll see you at the hunt. Take care."

And off he went to do his warm-ups and so

forth. Imagine him asking if I would "be hunting" with them! Who or whom did he think he was? Of course I would be hunting. It was MY ranch, after all.

Loper walked up just then. I gave him a big cowdog smile and barked, just to let him know that I was ready for the hunt.

"Now listen, pooch, we're going to be hunting behind a good dog today, and we don't need your kind of help."

HUH?

"And if you try to follow us, I'll have to tie you up. Now, you stay here and keep out of trouble, hear? Stay."

I didn't even try Heavy Begs. I knew it wouldn't work. What a lousy deal, confined to quarters on the first day of bird season and on my own ranch!

Loper joined the others and they hiked down into the brush and tall grass along Wolf Creek. They were not carrying shotguns, so it appeared that this was to be a practice day for the dog—who, of course, was out front and the center of attention, charging around in that Bird Dog Stealth pose of his.

If you ask me, he looked silly.

What's more, I didn't even care.

I hadn't planned on going anyway.

Too busy.

Show me a dog with a steady job and I'll show you a dog that doesn't have time to chase birds.

Phooey.

All at once I noticed that Drover was acting strangely. He was near the back of Billy's pickup. It appeared that he had fallen over backward and was kicking his legs in the air. Clearly, something was wrong with the little mutt and he needed my help.

I rushed to his side. "Drover, I saw the whole thing. You've been stricken with something terrible but don't panic. Lie still and give me your symptoms."

"Oh my gosh, thank goodness you made it! All at once I just lost control of my life."

"Exactly. I have a couple of theories on that, but first let's check out your vital signs. Heart?"

"Pounding like a drum."

"Hmm. What kind of drum?"

"Well, what are the choices? And hurry 'cause I think it's getting worse."

"Choices? Let's see: kettle drum, snare drum, bass drum, oil drum; bongos, congos, or kangaroos. Pick one, and hurry. I think you're getting worse."

"Yeah, I know. Kangaroos, 'cause my old heart's about to jump out of my chest."

I began pacing. "All right, Drover, your heart is jumping around like a kangaroo that is beating a drum. What color is the kangaroo?"

"Pink, with orange stripes."

"Hmmm. This is worse than I thought. How's your blood pressure?"

"I think it's a quart low."

"How about your vision?"

"Well, let's see. I thought I saw an angel in the back of Billy's pickup."

"Mercy. Was he playing a drum?"

"No, she was just sitting there."

"Hmmm. Give me a complete description. Facts, Drover, facts and details. No detail is too small to be large."

"Well, let's see here. She had . . ."

"Hold it right there. You said 'she.' Does that mean that she was a girl or a woman?"

"Yeah, I think so."

"Okay, go on. Finish your description of the angel."

"Well, she had pretty brown eyes and . . ."

"Whoa. Were the eyes pretty AND brown, or pretty brown? It could be important."

"Well, let's see. Both were both."

"You mean she had two eyes?"

"Oh yeah, and both of her two eyes were both

pretty and brown and pretty brown. And she had long flaxen hair, and I just fell in love with her nose."

I stared at the runt. "You're sicker than I thought, Drover. What kind of creep would fall in love with a nose?"

"Well, it was on her face and I loved her face too."

"Oh. Well, I think I've got this thing figgered out, Drover. The pieces of the puzzle have fallen into place at last."

"Oh good. What's happened to me?"

Once again, I began pacing back and forth in front of him. My mind seems to . . . I guess I've mentioned that before, but it's true.

"All right, Drover, listen carefully so that I don't have to repeat myself."

"What?"

"I said, listen repeatedly so that I don't have to care for myself."

"Gosh, are you sick too?"

"Hush, Drover. Number One, the angel you saw—or thought you saw—was actually a mental image of a kangaroo. Number Two, that would account for the odd kicking behavior of your heart."

"I'll be derned."

"But I'm not through. Number Three, your

mind produced this strange mental image because you are mentally pathetic."

"Gosh, you mean I can see things that other dogs can't see?"

"Exactly. In cases of mental pathetica, the vision of a kangaroo-angel is fairly common, but the important thing is that she was just a filament of your imagination."

"Oh good, I'm so happy. But there she is again."

I couldn't help chuckling. "Don't worry, son. On the count of three, I will clap my paws together and turn my eyes toward the Angelic Kangaroo and she will be gone. One. Two. And you will feel much better. Three!"

I clapped my paws together and turned my gaze toward the . . .

HUH?

. . . toward the angel, and holy smokes, there she was before my very eyes, the most gorgeous angel I had ever seen!

And she wasn't a kangaroo.

Forget the Kangaroo, It Was Beulah

Not only did she not look like a kangaroo, fellers, but she reminded me a whole lot of Miss Beulah the Collie.

All at once my heart was beating like a drum and jumping around inside my chest like a jack-rabbit. Or, okay, a kangaroo. My blood pressure suddenly felt a quart low. I fell over backward and began kicking my legs in the air.

Drover seemed to have suffered a relapse and was doing the same. No doubt an impartial observer would have found the scene a bit . . . uh . . . strange, two grown dogs doing such things, but an impartial observer would never have understood the incredible power of that woman's smile.

See, she had smiled at me! Holy smokes, how many nights had I dreamed of that very smile, and now here it was in front of me and it hit me like the Ray Gun of Love!

And then her soft collie voice came floating through the air and settled into the vast caverns of my eardrums: "Hello, boys. What on earth are you doing?"

See? She was wildly in love with me. Those were the words of a woman in love, the honey-dipped words of a collie princess who had forgotten about bird dogs and all the mistakes of the past!

At last I regained my footage and managed to speak to her in my smoothest, most charming voice.

"Hello, Beulah."

"Hello, Hank."

"It's been a long time."

"Yes, a long time."

"Until moments ago, I was a hermit living in the desert, eating cactus and grasshoppers. Now, you've brought rain and flowers, green grass and mud puddles."

"Oh my."

"Your face is just as lovely as ever, Miss Beulah. To quote the poet, 'Your face would sink a thousand ships.'"

She stared at me for a moment, then started laughing.

"That's very kind of you, but I think the poet meant to say *launch* a thousand ships, not sink them."

"Whatever. Has anyone ever told you what an awesome nose you have?"

She laughed again. "I don't think anyone has ever put it that way."

"Awesome nose, Beulah. If I had a nose like yours, I'd never get any work done. I'd just sit around looking at it, and then I'd be crosseyed."

"Well, I can't take any credit for my nose. I hope there are other qualities you like about me." Her expression darkened. "Is something wrong with Drover?"

He was still rolling around in the dirt.

"Who? Oh, him? No, he acts like this all the time. I think he's got worms. But back to your nose . . ."

At that very moment, the runt sat up and proceeded to butt into my business. "Beulah, I wrote a poem, just for you: 'Roses are red, chrysanthemums are violet/My heart's like an airplane, but the pilot bailed out.'"

Silence filled the air. Beulah blinked her eyes. I rolled mine. I was embarrassed. At last Beulah thought of something to say.

"Well, it's nice that you wrote a poem for me, Drover. Maybe you could work on it and make it even better."

I pushed myself in front of Drover. "Hey Beulah, speaking of poetry, it happens that I've composed a few verses myself. Get this: 'Roses are red, that's perfectly clear/Forget little Drover, he's a pain in the rear.'"

"Hank, that's not very nice."

"Okay, maybe you're right. Here's another one: 'Roses are red, your nose is just awesome/My heart's in a tree like an upside-down possum.'"

She stared at me. "I think I missed something."

"Well, possums wrap their tails around a tree limb and hang upside-down, don't you see, and . . . hey, it rhymed. Let's don't be too picky. I composed it on the spot. Give me a couple of days and . . ."

Her gaze had moved away from me and turned toward the creek. "Have they started yet? I wanted to watch Plato. He's worked so hard to get ready for bird season."

"Birds! Now there's a subject for a poem. Listen to this one, Beulah: 'Cardinals are red and bluebirds are blue/A dog who'd chase birds isn't worthy of you.'"

She didn't hear it, which was too bad. I thought it was even better than the one about possums. She moved to the front of the pickup bed to get a better view of the bird-chaser . . . uh, Plato, that is.

Down on the ground, I followed her around to the side of the pickup. "Hey Beulah, have I ever showed you my tricks? Watch this one."

I stood on my back legs and walked forward three steps. She gave me a glance and a quick smile. "That's nice, Hank." Then she turned her eyes back to the creek.

"Nice but not nice enough, huh? Okay, check this one out." This time, I walked on my back legs AND moved my front paws. "What do you think now? Have you ever seen a better trick?"

"That's a good one," she said, but she hardly even looked at me.

"Okay, this next one will turn your head, Beulah. Watch this. Before your very eyes, I will stand on my back legs, do a complete back flip, and land on my feet again. You ready?"

Ah ha, at last I had her attention. I pushed up on my hind legs, went into a deep crouch, sprang upward with all my might, negotiated a very difficult backward flip maneuver in midair, and . . .

BONK!

. . . more or less landed on my head, you might say. Remember, it was a very difficult trick. Very few dogs could have pulled it off, or would have even attempted it.

Did it hurt? You bet it did. For a moment there, I saw checkers and stars and red billygoats. As I staggered to my feet, I suddenly realized that (1) my neck was bent and (2) someone was laughing at my misfortune.

With great difficulty, I turned my crooked neck and injured head toward the sound of the laughter. It appeared to be coming from my Collie Princess, who had thrust a paw over her mouth to hide her amusement, only the paw-covering-up deal hadn't worked.

Her laughter came spilling out. "Oh Hank, I'm sorry. I don't mean to laugh, but sometimes you do the most ridiculous things."

"Yes, I've noticed, and they always seem to happen when you're around."

"Well, maybe you're trying too hard. Sometimes it's better just to relax and let things happen in their own time."

I thought about that. "So what you're saying is that if I stop trying to impress you, you might be impressed? That doesn't make sense, Beulah."

She smiled and shrugged. "But it happens that way. We can't control the way we feel."

"Well, let me try this out on you. Suppose, just suppose for the sake of supposing, that I burst into song at this very moment, and the song happened to speak to this very issue. Would it win me points or lose me points?"

She cast a quick glance toward the south, where her bird dog friend was beginning the hunt. "I can't say, Hank. You'd just have to try it and see."

The Punt of Love

How can I begin to tell you, my pet,
The depths of my utter confusion.
You tell me go slow, I tell me go fast,
I think that I need a transfusion
Of daring ideas or something that works,
Explaining a lady dog's mind.
I tried all my tricks and fell on my head
And now I'm just further behind.

Now, let us be frank, go straight to the point,
I've tried and I've tried to impress you.
The harder I try, the harder I fall,
It's finally time to address you,
To ask you, what gives? What's going on here?

And what in the heck you expect
A feller to think or say or do,
Just short of breaking his neck?

I fervently wish, I fondly desire
That someone would draw me a map
That showed the terrain of a lady dog's
mind,
Every highway and mountain and gap,
And valleys and streams and swamps and
plains.
I think such a product would sell.
But I'd probably need a compass or three
And radar devices as well.

So what can I say? We're back to square one.
The tide has come into the shore.
I've squared the circle and circled the square.
I'm just as confused as before.
The answer, I fear, is simple and plain,
There isn't a tonic or stunt;
There isn't a map or even a clue.
The only solution is . . . punt.

Well, I belted out my song and waited to see what she would say. She had listened to the whole thing, and now I caught a glimpse of her smiling.

I wasn't sure what that meant, but smiling was probably better than some of the alternatives.

At last she spoke. "Well, Hank, it seems you have a hard time understanding us girls."

"Yes ma'am, I certainly do."

"Well," she dropped her voice to a whisper, "sometimes we have trouble understanding us too."

"Uh-oh. You mean, you don't have any more answers than I do?" She shook her head. I slapped my forehead with my left paw—and, ouch, jarred my almost-broken neck. "Oh brother, this is even worse than I thought. Where do we go from here?"

She heaved a sigh and looked up at the clouds. "Why don't you jump up here and we'll watch the hunt together. We'll worry about the rest of it later."

Well . . . watching bird dogs wasn't my idea of great fun, but sitting in the back of a pickup with the most gorgeous collie gal in all of Texas . . . hmmm, that was no bad deal.

A guy never knew what might happen.

Tall oats from tiny acorns grow.

Heh, heh.

She Resists My Charms

Oaks, not oats. Mighty oaks from tiny acorns grow.

Anyways, it appeared that the winds of love had shifted and Beulah was craving my company. (It must have been my song that did the trick. Pretty good song, huh?)

All at once I felt fresh energy and a new zest for life galloping through my entire system. I shrugged off the terrible injury to my neck and head, and sprang like a deer into the back of the pickup.

Beulah was impressed. I could see that at a glance. Hey, no bird dog in history had ever jumped into a pickup with such grace and so forth.

But wouldn't you know it? As soon as Drover saw me back there with Miss Beulah—and Beulah about to faint from the excitement of having me at her side—when Little Stub Tail saw all this, he was suddenly cured of his childish spasms.

He began running around in circles and tried several times to climb over the tail-end gate. He failed, of course, but managed to leave several scratch marks on Billy's pickup.

"Hank, wait, I want up there too!"

I gave him a withering glare. "I'm afraid not, son. Two's a company and three's a corporation. Beulah and I need some time alone . . ." I gave her a sly wink. ". . . and this would be an excellent time for you to do something constructive. For example, you might want to go chase your tail."

"Yeah, but I don't have a tail. It got chopped off when I was a pup."

"Life is hard, Drover, and often unfair. Be glad they chopped off your tail and not your head. And above all, scram."

"Yeah, but I want to be with Beulah. I think she likes me."

"She's just being polite, Drover."

"Oh drat."

"And we'll have no more of your naughty language. Now, run along, and have a good day."

He whined and moaned and went padding off to the gas tanks. I watched him for a moment and took note of a rather important detail: He wasn't limping.

Well, having disposed of Drover and his . . . imagine him thinking that Beulah liked HIM . . . I turned to the Lady of My Dreams, wiggled my eyebrows, and . . . HUH? It appeared that she had, uh, moved to the front and was watching the sporting event, so to speak. I joined her.

"Sorry to keep you waiting, my lamb, but I had to take care of some unfinished business."

Her eyes swung around to me. They were sparkling. "He's working."

"What?"

"Plato."

"Oh. Yes. Him."

"He's out in front of the men, and look at him go!"

I tossed a glance toward the Birdly Wonder, and two words rushed to my mind: Big Deal. Of course I didn't say this aloud. I knew that Beulah had some slight affection for the creep . . . uh, for the bird dog . . . for Plato, shall we say, and I didn't wish to scoff at the utter stupidity of his . . .

I didn't want to poke fun at his occupation, is the point.

"You know, Beulah, I'm fairly affluent in birding myself."

"How nice."

I took this opportunity to move a bit closer to her. Heh, heh. "Perhaps you weren't aware of that."

"No."

"But it's true. The study of birds is called 'Birdathology,' from the root-word 'bird' and the rootless-word 'athology.'"

She scooted away from me and said, "Shhhh."

"Sorry." We watched in silence for several minutes. "He doesn't seem to be finding any quail." I scootched over in her direction.

"He will. He always does. Just watch."

She scootched over to the east. Gee, the way she was squirming around, she must have been as bored as I was.

I tried to concentrate on the exciting events that were unfolding along the creek—Plato streaking back and forth with his nose to the ground and his tail stuck straight out behind him.

Big deal. I was dying of boredom.

"Beulah, I must tell you something very important. It's going to come as a terrible shock."

That worked. She tore her gaze away from the hunt.

"What?"

"Well, Beulah, I happen to know that your friend . . . Plato, that is, won't find any birds along the creek. I monitor the comings and goings of our quail population rather closely, you see, and I happen to know . . ."

"Oh look! He's found something."

I narrowed my eyes and studied the scene. Sure enough, Plato had locked down into a pointing position, as though he had been transformed into a cement statue.

I took this opportunity to move a bit closer to her warm side.

"Beulah, I hate to be the messenger of bad

news, but I've been through that creek bottom dozens of times, hundreds of times, and know every grain of sand and every sprig of grass, and I've never seen a quail down there. I'm sorry. I know he's a friend of yours, but . . ."

WHIRRRRRR!

Birds? Twenty or thirty quail?

She turned to me with a smile. "See? I knew he'd find birds." She scooted east.

I found myself coughing. "Yes, I also thought he might stumble across that one covey . . . we've been watching it for, uh, weeks now and . . ."

Down below, I heard the men shouting, "Good dog, Plato! Nice work, boy."

Okay, so maybe he'd lucked into finding the only covey of quail along that section of the creek. Any mutt could find one covey. The real test would come in finding another—and I knew for a fact that there wasn't one.

And just to prove it, I scooted a bit closer to . . . my goodness, she had lovely brown eyes!

"Beulah, I'm a dog of few words, so let's go straight to the bottom line. I think the time has come for you to . . ."

"He's picked up another scent. See how he's slowed down?"

"It's a rabbit, Beulah. Don't get your hopes up.

But as I was saying, I'm a dog of few words."

"Good."

"So we agree on that. The problem with dogs these days is that they talk too much."

"Uh-huh."

"And what I have to say won't take long. You see, I think our relationship has reached a turning point, and the time has come, my buttercup, for you to . . ."

"Hank, I keep hearing your voice."

"That's wonderful news, my cactus flower, because I often hear yours—in my dreams."

"Yes, but this is no dream."

"Oh, it could be, my little bluebonnet. Our fondest dreams are within our grasp. All we have to do is . . ."

"Shhh. Look, he's on point again."

"Who? Oh, him." Sure enough, What's-His-Name had turned to stone once again. "You know, he's going to get in trouble for pointing those rabbits. But as I was saying . . ."

WHIRRRR!

By George, the weeds just came alive with whirring wings and flying birds. Beulah turned to me and smiled.

"As you were saying?"

"Beulah, I don't think those were actually quail.

They looked more like, uh, blackbirds or starlings. Really."

"They were quail."

"Okay, maybe they were quail, but they were stupid quail. A smart quail would be up in the sand draws, where it belongs."

"A quail is a quail."

"I never denied that."

"And Plato found them. It won't hurt you to admit that he's good at his work."

"Okay, fine. I'll admit that he's one lucky bird dog."

"Hank."

"And he's pretty good at his line of work, although . . ."

"Hank, shh. Let's watch."

We turned our respective eyes to the south and watched The Hero at work. He was running again, sniffing out every bush and clump of grass.

Hadn't we seen all this before?

I was getting restless. My time with Beulah was slipping away. I decided to make my move.

I scootched myself closer, ever closer, to her warm wonderful side and . . . my goodness, we must have run out of room on her side of the . . . she more or less fell out of the back of the . . . uh, pickup, you might say.

"Oh dear," I said, looking down at her as she picked herself up off the ground. "You fell out . . . I guess."

She beamed a rather hostile gaze in my direction. "You pushed me out!"

"It was an accident, Beulah, honest. I just wanted . . ."

"You wanted my attention, but you can't have it. Don't you understand? I want to watch Plato at work."

"No, I don't understand that. You have a cowdog right here beside you, so how could you have any interest in a bird dog? It doesn't make sense, Beulah."

She sighed and shook her head. "I can't explain it, and even if I could, you wouldn't accept it."

"Would you like me better if I ran around chasing birds? Okay, if that's what it takes, that's what I'll do. Good-bye, Beulah, I'm going away to prove that I'm a better bird dog than Plato. When I return, you'll see the truth at last."

"Oh Hank, honestly!"

I leaped out of the pickup and stormed away. She tried to call me back but by then my heart had turned to purest stone.

I left her alone with her tears and memories, and went in search of Pete the Barncat.

A Major Theft on the Ranch

Why would I go looking for Pete? Good question. Under ordinary circumstances I wouldn't have, but it just happened that in my last conversation with the little sneak, he had said something about "impressing Beulah the Collie," if I recalled his words exactly.

I had to find out what he meant by that.

Don't get me wrong. I wasn't in the habit of seeking the advice of cats, but Pete was an expert on sneaky plans and I needed some kind of special sneaky plan to take Beulah's mind off her bird dog friend.

It was for her own good, don't you see. She needed the help of a true friend.

I knew where to find the cat. In the middle of

the day, he hung out on the shady side of the house, in the iris patch, to be exact. There, he lurked and waited and stared out at the rest of the world with his big yellow eyes.

What was he waiting and lurking for? Scraps. A helpless bird. A leg to rub on. Who knows why cats spend so much of their time lurking? It's just their nature to lurk in sneaky places.

I felt very uncomfortable as I made my way past the gas tanks and up the hill behind the house, as though I were going into a den of thieves. I found myself glancing over both shoulders, and hoping that no one was watching.

If word ever got out that I had gone to Pete for advice, my career would be finished.

I didn't leap over the fence and enter Sally May's precious yard, for obvious reasons. Dogs were forbidden and I had no wish to tangle with the lady of the house. Sally May and I had suffered our share of misunderstandings, don't you know, and I had no wish to throw gasoline on that open wound.

We had been getting along pretty well, see, and I wanted to keep it that way.

I sneaked past the yard gate and around to the north side. From that vantage point, I could see him—Pete, that is—hunkered down and lurking in the irises.

I tossed a glance over my shoulder and dropped my voice to a whisper. "Pssst! Pete, come here."

His eyes swung around. He was grinning. "Hi Hankie. How's the quail hunting?"

"Not too swell, Kitty. Come over here to the fence."

"But I'm so comfortable, Hankie. I just love to lie here in the shade and watch the world go by."

"I know, but this is important. Come."

He ran his tongue over his left paw. "But Hankie, you haven't said the magic word. I can't move until you say it."

I noticed that my lips were beginning to rise into a snarl, but I shut them down just in time. "I don't know any magic words."

"Well just darn the luck. I can't move until I hear the magic word."

I gritted my teeth. "Okay, magic word. Abracadabra?"

"Nope. You missed. Try again."

"Try again, magic word . . . okay, I think I've got it: shazzam." He shook his head. "Pete, that's a perfectly good magic word."

"I know, Hankie, but it's not the right one. Keep trying. I've got all day."

Once again, I glanced over both shoulders. So far, I hadn't been spotted. "Okay, Pete, I've got it this time. It's slightly longer than one word but it ought to work."

"Well, give it a try and we'll see."

"Here we go: Come here immediately, and that's a direct order from the Head of Ranch Security."

He shook his head. "Won't work, Hankie, but I'll give you a hint. It's a six-letter word that begins with P and ends with E, and it's one of the most powerful words in the world."

I ran all that through Data Control. "How about a five letter word that begins with P and ends in D? Pound, as in 'If you don't get your carcass over here this very minute, I'll pound you into the ground like a tent stake.'"

"No, no. You're getting it all wrong, Hankie, and I guess I'll have to tell you. The magic word is . . ." His eyes popped open like two big moons. ". . . 'please.'"

I stared at him in disbelief. "Please? You think I'm going to say . . . ha, ha, no I don't think so, Kitty. I came here to do a little business with you, but I can't do business with a cat who's totally unreasonable. Sorry, Pete, I'll just take my deal down the street."

"Bye, Hankie."

I turned and marched away. "See you around, Kitty. Too bad for you. You'll be sorry, of course, but . . ." I turned and marched back to the fence. "Pete, will you please come over here so that we can talk?"

"Hmmmm. What was the magic word again?"

"Please. There, I've said it twice."

He lifted a paw and slapped at an iris leaf. "You know, Hankie, if you'd said it right away, I think 'please' would have been good enough. But you didn't, so maybe you should say . . . 'pretty please with sugar on top.'"

I glared at him. "What? Pretty please with . . . no, I will never say that to a cat, never! Sorry, Pete, you're just . . ." I turned and marched away. "You're being totally unreasonable about this and . . ." I stopped and marched back to the fence. "All right, Pete, one of us has to walk the extra mile, so . . . pretty please with sugar on top."

I almost choked on those words.

He grinned, pushed himself up, stretched each of his four legs, and took his sweet time about ambling over to where I was standing—and waiting. First thing, he started rubbing on the fence between us.

"All right, Hankie. What can I do for you?"

Again, I glanced around to be sure that nobody was watching this. "Pete, I hate doing business with creeps like you."

"I know you do, Hankie. It probably just kills your cowdog pride. But living in Plato's shadow hurts even worse, doesn't it, Hankie? I mean, he's doing so well with the quail, and everyone is so impressed."

I beamed him a glare of laser beams. "You think you know everything, don't you? Well, you don't. There are many things you don't know, but yes, you seem to have scored a bull's eye on this deal, so let's go straight to the point."

"The point." He rolled over on his back and rubbed around in the dirt. "What could the point be, Hankie?"

"You know what I want. Quit stalling."

"Let's see if I can guess, Hankie. Could it be that you want my advice on how to impress Miss Beulah?"

I glanced around. Nobody was listening. "That's correct."

"Hmmm. Some heroic act that might pull her attention away from her bird dog friend?"

"Yes, and get on with it. This hurts me more than you can imagine."

"Ohhhhhhh, poor doggie."

He rolled over on his belly, pushed up on all fours, and shook the dust and grass off his coat. Then he turned to me with those weird cattish eyes.

"Hankie, did you happen to notice that Sally May put out a bucket of corn this morning?"

"No, I missed that, Pete, and to be frank about it, corn doesn't interest me much."

"I understand, Hankie. You're a very busy dog."

"Right, and corn doesn't fit into my . . . why did she put out a bucket of corn? I mean, that doesn't make any sense."

"I know, Hankie, that's exactly what I thought. Do you suppose she set it out to dry?"

"Maybe. Could be. Yes, I suppose that's as good an explanation as any. She was drying her corn, and so what?"

"Well, she set out a bucket of corn in the pasture, maybe fifty yards in front of the yard gate."

"Fifty yards. Got it. Go on."

"It was in the sun, so I assumed she was drying the corn."

"Sun. Drying. Got it. Keep truckin'."

"But then . . . well, it must have been while you were asleep . . ."

"Objection. I wasn't totally asleep. Keep your opinions out of this, Kitty, and stick to the facts. Go on."

"Well, while you were lying down and resting your eyes . . ."

"Yes, yes? We're getting close to something, Pete, I can feel it."

"While you were resting, a bunch of wild turkeys came up from the creek bottom and . . ."

"Turkeys, wild turkeys. Okay."

". . . came out of the creek bottom and, well, I'd hate to jump to hasty conclusions, Hankie, but it certainly appeared to me that they were stealing Sally May's corn."

That word sent a shock throughout my entire body. I stared at the cat for a long time, wondering if he knew what an important piece of information he had just given me.

No, of course he didn't. He was just a dumb

cat—overweight, overbearing, and over the hill.

But I knew, and suddenly a clever plan began taking shape in the vast caverns of my mind.

Oh yes, and at that very moment Drover showed up.

A Plan Takes Shape in My Mind

He sat down beside us and gave me his usual silly grin. “Hi Hank. I guess I fell asleep. Did I miss anything?”

“You missed everything, Drover. I’ve just blown this case wide open.”

“I’ll be derned. Which case?”

“The Case of the Turkey Bandits, and if you want to learn more about it, just sit and watch.”

“Yeah, ’cause a potted watch never boils.”

I stared at the runt. “What?”

“I said . . . I’m not sure what I said.”

“Something about ‘boils.’ ”

“Oh yeah. I had a boil once, right on my hiney.”

“I’m sure that was very painful, Drover, but this is not the time or the place to discuss it.”

"I couldn't sit down for a whole week."

"I'm in the midst of a very important interrogation, so please hush."

At last he hushed and I whirled back to the cat. I couldn't keep an evil smile from forming on my lips. My patience had been rewarded. At last I had this cat exactly where he wanted me.

He was watching. "You're smiling, Hankie. Did I say something funny?"

"It's an inside joke, Pete. I don't think you'd understand and I don't have time to explain it. Sorry. You can run along now. I've completed my interrogation."

"Oh? But Hankie, I thought you wanted my advice."

I burst out laughing. "Advice? Me, take advice from a cat? Ha! You must have me confused with some other dog."

"But Hankie, you said . . ."

"Hey Pete, we've been watching those thieving turkeys for days and weeks, just waiting for the right moment to spring my trap."

"My goodness, Hankie, I'm impressed."

"You should be, Kitty, but wait until you hear the entire plan. It will blow your doors off."

"Mercy, and I don't even have any doors."

"Exactly." I began pacing. "Okay, Pete, listen

closely. Don't you get it? Those turkeys were STEALING Sally May's corn, and they were doing it in daily broadlight!"

Pete let out a gasp. "My goodness, Hankie, I never would have thought of that."

"Ha! Of course not, but that's why I'm here, Pete, and that's why you chose to bring this information to the Head of Ranch Security. You came to the right place, pal, and even though you won't get any credit for it, you and I will know that you played a small but insignificant part in saving Sally May's corn from the thieving turkeys."

"Oh thank you, Hankie." He studied the claws in his left paw. "Will you have to . . . well, chase the turkeys away? Run them off and bark at them?"

I gave him a wink and a smile. "Hey Kitty, you're starting to catch on. Keep it up and I may find a little job for you."

"Oh my, wouldn't that be fun!" He grinned at me and batted his eyelids several times. "But don't you think you should wait until the Famous Bird Dog comes? Turkeys are birds, you know, and you're not a bird dog."

"Hey Pete, that brings us to Part Two of my two-part plan." I stopped pacing and stuck my nose right in his face. "Beulah seems to be impressed by bird dogs, right? Turkeys are birds, right? I save

Sally May's precious corn from the thieving turkeys, win her total devotion, and . . . Miss Beulah watches the whole adventure from her box seat in the pickup. Is that an awesome plan or what?"

Get this. Pete was so overwhelmed and blown away by my awesome plan that he fell over on his side. "Oh Hankie, you may be a genius."

"I'm glad you finally realize that, Pete, and I'm sorry it took you so long. It's called Getting Two Bird Dogs With One Stone. You stay here and watch, because somebody on this ranch is fixing to learn a painful lesson."

"I'll bet on that."

I was all set to go streaking off on my mission, my very important mission of breaking up the gang of Turkey Bandits, when all at once Drover spoke.

"Hank, wait, there's something I've got to tell you! It's a trap."

I throttled back on my rocket engines and stared at the little mutt. "What's a trap?"

"The turkeys and the corn. It's a trap."

Pete and I exchanged secret smiles. "Drover, it's too bad that you chose to sleep through the briefing and the planning session for this mission."

"Yeah but . . ."

"Don't interrupt. The mission has already

begun. In fact, we're in the Countdown Phase at this very moment. You have about fifteen seconds to state your case, if you have one."

"Oh my gosh, I hope I can . . . let me think here. Corn. Sally May put out some corn."

"We're aware of that, Drover, and don't bother to tell us that the turkeys are stealing it, because we know that too."

"But Hank, it's a trap. See, Sally May was trying to . . . EEEE-YOW!"

That was odd. All at once, Pete stuck his paw through the hogwire fence and delivered a handful of claws to Drover's tail section. The little mutt jumped straight up into the air and took refuge behind me.

"Hank, did you see that? He slapped me!"

Pete blinked his eyes and grinned. "Well, just darn the luck. My claws went off, like a loaded mousetrap. Maybe that was the trap he was talking about, Hankie."

"Hmmm, yes. It does fit, doesn't it?"

"Yes it does, and his fifteen seconds are up, Hankie, and you'd better go save Sally May's corn."

"Good thinking, Kitty."

Drover was hopping around like a . . . I don't know what. A grasshopper, I suppose, a grasshopper that kept repeating the same meaningless phrase: "Yeah-but, yeah-but, yeah-but!"

"Drover, try to control yourself. You're embarrassing me."

"Yeah but . . ."

"I'm about to leave on a very important mission."

"Yeah but . . ."

"And will you stop saying that? You're driving me nuts."

"Yeah but . . ."

"Okay, pal, that did it! Go to your room immediately and stay there for fifteen minutes."

"Yeah but . . ."

"Thirty minutes. An hour? Two weeks? What does it take?"

"A trap!"

"Okay, fine. Go sit in a trap for thirty minutes. I'll look you up when I've finished with these thieving turkeys." I pushed him aside and throttled up my engines. "See you later, Pete, and thanks for the tip."

And with that, I hit Full Throttle on all engines and went roaring off to intercept the enemy.

Sally May would be SO PROUD! Whether Pete knew it or not, he had given me a great opportunity to pile up some Goodie Points with the lady of the house. You might recall that our relationship had experienced its share of . . . well, ups and downs, shall we say.

Tiny misunderstandings that had grown into something fairly serious. Sometimes, when she looked at me and one side of her upper lip rose into a snarl, I even got the feeling . . . well, that she just didn't like me.

And I, being a very sensitive dog beneath all the muscle and bone and hair and so forth, had almost worried myself sick about it, had hardly been able to sleep for weeks and . . .

Okay, I'd caught myself a little nap that very afternoon, but only because sheer exhaustion had finally dragged me down.

But the point is that I was now on a mission to save her precious corn from marauding bands of wild turkeys. You see, that bucket contained the family's entire supply of food for the winter.

Yes. She was drying it, preserving it for the long cold winter months—months of wind and snow and snowy wind, months when her precious children would wake up in the morning, cold and hungry and crying for bowls of dried corn.

Gee, I sure hoped that Baby Molly grew some more teeth. She only had three or four teeth, and she would need a pretty good set to chew up that dried corn.

Even horses have trouble chewing dried corn.

Well, by the time I roared past the trees in the shelter belt, bending them almost to the ground in the wake of my powerful engines, I had worked myself up into towering rage.

Anyone who would steal food from innocent children would have to deal with Hank the Cowdog.

Zooming south from the shelter belt, I began picking them up on VIZRAD (Visual Radar). Holy smokes, I'd never seen so many wild turkeys in one bunch. There must have been fifty of them!

Whole families. All sizes and shapes. Hens, toms, and whatever you call the young'uns. Squabs? Chicks? Poults? Turklings?

It didn't matter what they called themselves. To me they were all thieves and robbers, and their actions were proving it. They were pushing and shoving and fighting for the right to steal Sally May's entire winter ration of food.

They would pay for their greed and gluttony, and fellers, I was going to enjoy collecting the rent.

I Arrest the Thieving Turkeys

Thirty yards out, I locked in on the five biggest gluttonyest birds. They had pushed the rest out of the way and were gobbling corn. At twenty yards, I began arming Tooth Cannons and Barkolasers.

By this time, several of the turkey elders heard me coming. They lifted their heads and began clucking. The others stopped their pecking and so forth and pointed in my direction. They knew *something* was fixing to happen, but they didn't know exactly what.

They were growing restless, moving around in that long awkward trot of theirs—turkey trot, I suppose you'd call it. They have long skinny legs, don't you know, and the legs are hinged backward at the knee. They look pretty silly when they bounce along, like camels or something, and the faster they walk the sillier they look.

Ten yards out, I reached for the Firing Button and . . . was that a voice coming from the direction of the house? A human voice? Yes, there it was again.

"Hank, don't you dare . . . !"

It seemed to be the voice of Sally May who seemed to be standing out on the front porch. Amidst the roar of the wind and my rocket engines, I couldn't hear everything she was saying but I pretty muchly knew. She was cheering me on to battle but also worrying that I might get hurt.

Good old Sally May, always concerned about the safety of her dogs and children. That's a mother for you. Instead of fretting over the loss of her precious supply of winter corn, she was worried sick about . . . well, ME, you might say.

Pretty touching, huh?

It almost brought tears to my eyes.

Just knowing that she REALLY CARED made it all worthwhile—the sacrifice, the danger, the tremendous effort, and, yes, the fun. I'll admit that I was having fun.

Five yards away from Point Zero, I was ready to scatter some birds. I opened up with Full Barkolasers and went smashing and crashing right into the middle of the villains.

My goodness, you never saw such flapping or heard such clucking and squawking! I mean, I had scattered more than my share of chickens but this was my first attempt at plowing through a herd of turkeys.

Fellers, if a dog enjoys running through chickens, he will absolutely LOVE bulldozing turkeys. I mean, the noise and the action that turkeys produce are guaranteed to give a ranch dog the biggest thrill of his life.

It's like chickens multiplied by ten.

It was wonderful! There for a few seconds, I experienced the total thrill of . . . hmm, power, I suppose—the pure raw power of an angry ranch dog administering Ranch Justice.

I loved it, the squawking and flapping. Ho, ho! Feathers flew and so did birds, feathers and birds flying off in all directions like an explosion of, well, feathers and birds.

Hey, I felt so wild and excited about this deal that I zoomed in and grabbed the biggest tom turkey in the bunch, put the old Cowdog Fanglock on his . . .

BIFF! BONK! POW!

. . . wing, and the thing you never hear about

wild turkeys is that you should never try to grab one. Remember those long skinny legs? They look pretty funny until they're in your face and bread-box, and that's when you realize that wild turkeys are a whole lot tougher and meaner than your average chicken.

No comparison.

Turkeys stay wild and alive by kicking, gouging, clawing, pecking, and wing-thrashing anything foolish enough to take hold of them. In the first five seconds, I had the turkey. Over the next two minutes, which seemed like two hours, he had ME, and fellers, I thought I never would get away from that stupid . . .

I, uh, gave him a stern dose of Ranch Justice and hurried back to the house.

Actually, I limped back to the house, but at a high rate of speed, while throwing barks over my shoulder.

It was pretty clear by then that I had chosen to jump the wrong guy, a Green Beret commando with five black belts in Turkey Karate.

He wanted Sally May's precious corn? Fine. He could be my guest. He could eat all the stupid corn he wanted—canned corn, creamed corn, corn on the cob, popcorn, I didn't care what kind of corn he ate, and I hoped he choked on it too.

The dumb bird. I had a claw mark for every piece of corn in the bucket. And bruised ribs. And a gash on the end of my nose.

I limped to the yard gate. There, I turned and looked back toward the corn bucket. All the turkeys had fled to the creek, even the cheating bully who had . . . even the bully cheater I had beaten to a pulp.

I paused at the yard gate and gave them one last withering barrage of barking. "Let that be a lesson to you! Just remember that you're nothing but a bunch of turkeys with skinny legs!"

Pretty impressive, huh? Yes sir, I got 'em told, and then I turned back to the . . .

A long shadow had fallen across the ground in front of me. It bore some resemblance to the form of a . . . well, of a human, perhaps of the female variety. My keen eyes scanned the shadow from left to right, moving from the top to the bottom, and there I noticed . . .

Hmmm, a pair of red roper boots, and these were not shadows but rather real actual boots. My eyes moved upward from the boots, following what appeared to be a pair of jeans that might very well have contained . . . legs.

My gaze paused at the alleged waist. There, I observed a pair of hands that seemed to be, uh, jammed upon the waistline, in a manner that suggested . . . oops.

I had seen such hands jammed upon such a waistline before, and those had never been what you would call . . . happy occasions, so to speak.

Suddenly my mouth felt dry. My tail began to sink between my legs and I noticed that my head was dropping to the angle that expressed . . . well, sorrow and regret, my deepest and most sincere sorrow and regret.

It was only then that I dared to roll my eyes upward, so as to confirm my suspicion that the figure looming above me belonged to . . .

Yikes, what a face! The mouth was as thin and stiff as a nail. The eyes were like two blasts from a blue norther and they sent shivers tumbling down my spinebone.

Ho boy. It appeared that we had us another, uh, breakdown in communications.

I tapped the last five inches of my tail on the ground, very slowly: tap, tap, tap. And I threw my last reserves of energy into gathering up a smile of utter sincerity, as if to say, "Hey, Sally May, how's it going?"

Gulp.

She didn't speak. Instead, her nostrils flared so much that, all of a sudden, they resembled the head of a rattlesnake, a merciless diamondback rattlesnake that was about to strike.

I felt my body sinking to the ground. With luck, I would sink to a depth of about six feet and then pull the hole in behind me.

This was serious, I could tell. But what had I done? My mind raced back over the events of the past two weeks and came up with . . . nothing. Nothing but hard work and the purest of intentions.

Sincerity. Courtesy, kindness, obedience, reverence.

Maybe she had the wrong dog, a simple case of, uh, mistaken identity.

A terrible silence loomed between us, like a poisonous yellow cloud of sulphurous sulphur. At last she spoke.

"You . . . you . . . you nincompoop! It's taken me two weeks to get those turkeys to come up to feed. Finally they came out of the brush and what did you do? *You ran right through the middle of them and scared them away!*"

Yes, but they were eating your . . .

"Do you think we need to be protected from our wildlife? No, you bonehead, we enjoy WATCHING the wildlife, because they're pretty and they're majestic, and I like pretty things and . . ."

She shook her head and rolled her eyes. "You are so dumb, SO DUMB! I can't believe you'd do this to me. We buy you dog food and give you a nice home, and this is the thanks we get."

She glared down at me, looked away, muttered something under her breath, and glared down at me again.

"Protecting us from the wild turkeys! You . . . I

just . . . sometimes I . . . you're the . . . ohhhhhhh!" She stamped her foot and bent down so that her face was only inches away from mine. "Listen, buster, if you ever chase my turkeys again . . ."

I stopped breathing and waited to hear the next blast of threats, but nothing came. Instead . . . footsteps? Loud footsteps?

Someone was running toward us. Sally May tore her gaze away from me, and I seized the opportunity to vanish into the shrubberies beneath her living room window.

I thought I was all alone, but imagine my surprise when I saw a grinning face right there beside me. It belonged to Pete.

"Why you little pest, you led me right into a trap!"

"Now Hankie, don't be bitter. It served you right for running me up a tree."

"Oh yeah? Well, I'm fixing to do worse than that, Kitty."

"Ah, ah, ah. Better not, Hankie. If you so much as raise your voice at me, I'll cry and squeal and go limping over to Sally May, and you know the rest."

He was smirking and batting his eyes, and I could hardly contain my desire to smash him up like . . . I don't know what. China in a bull shop, I suppose.

"Are you trying to threaten me, Pete?"

"Um-hm. Is it working?"

"Ha. Threats never work on me, Kitty, but it just happens that I'm too busy to give you your daily thrashing, so you lucked out."

"Whatever works, Hankie."

Having disposed of the cat with my slashing wit, I turned my attention toward whomever or whatever had made the loud footsteps I had heard.

It was Loper.

Gulp. My goose appeared to be cooked.

Beulah Is Kidnapped by a Cannibal!

I could hear Loper and Sally May talking in low voices. Now and then my name came up.

Out of the corner of my eye, I caught a glimpse of Pete. He was bathing his left front paw with a long pink tongue, and every time my name was mentioned, he gave me a wink and a smile.

I was in deep trouble, fellers, and the cat was loving every minute of it.

Slim and Billy joined the Kangaroo Court. Oh yes, and the bird dog was there too. It was sounding worse by the minute. In sheer desperation, I began digging. If they talked long enough, maybe I could dig a tunnel . . .

"Hank! Come here." That was Loper's voice.

They had all turned and were looking toward my . . . what I had supposed was my hiding place. Gulp.

I shot a glance at Kitty-Kitty. "Bye, Hankie. I'll always remember the good times we had together."

"Hank, come here!"

Well, it appeared that I had come to the end of my road. I'd had a good life. I rose from the shrubberies and crept out, a picture of shame and disgrace. I felt their eyes on me as I slinked over to Loper and fell down at his feet.

HUH?

He bent down and rubbed me on the ears and said—you won't believe this, I sure didn't—and he said, "Good dog, Hank. Good dog."

I gazed up at the circle of faces and . . . my goodness, they were all smiling! What the . . .

Sally May knelt down and took my head in her hands and began stroking my ears. "Hank, I'm sorry I was hateful to you, but I didn't see the coyote."

Coyote?

Loper gave me a scratch on the head. "Yeah, if old Hank hadn't come charging out when he did, that coyote would have had himself a turkey dinner. Good dog, Hank."

Ohhhhh, the coyote. Yes, of course, the, uh, sneaking murderous coyote who had tried to tamper with our precious turkey wildlifes.

I looked around the circle of smiling faces, whapped my tail on the ground, and gave them my biggest cowdog smile.

Just then Plato came bounding up. "By golly, Hank, that was really something, the way you took after that coyote. And he was a big rascal too. I don't know how you did that, Hank."

I tried to appear humble. "Oh, it was no big deal, just part of my job. Some of us point quail and some of us beat up coyotes."

"No kidding? You beat him up? I wasn't close enough to see the whole thing."

"Oh yeah, we had quite a scuffle." I pointed to the scratch on my nose. "He landed a few lucky punches but I pretty well thrashed him. I don't think he'll be back for a while."

"What a guy! And I guess you weren't even scared, huh?"

I couldn't help chuckling. "Scared, of one huge enormous coyote? Nah. It was just a routine call."

"Wow."

Just then, I noticed that the conversation above me had stopped. Billy had turned around and was looking off toward the creek.

"She's not in the pickup. I don't know where she could be. Beulah! Here, gal."

Plato and I traded glances. Then Slim said, "You don't reckon she went down to the creek to get a drink, do you?"

Billy shook his head. "Boy, I hope not. She's no fightin' dog and that coyote . . . boys, I think we'd better find my collie."

"Let's take these two dogs. They can pick up the scent."

HUH?

Plato and I happened to be looking at each other at that very moment. I noticed that his eyes crossed and his jaw dropped several inches. Perhaps mine did too. I mean, I'd already whipped my coyotes for the day and . . .

The men headed south toward the creek. "Come on, dogs! Out front. Get those noses to the ground. Find Beulah. Find the coyote."

Plato was the first to speak. "Hank, there's something I must tell you."

"Right, and there's something I'd like to mention to you, Plato. You see . . ."

"Come on dogs, let's go!"

Gulp.

It appeared that we had been summoned for active duty. I took the lead and loped out into that grassy flat just south of the house. Plato came along behind. We spread out in front of the men, put our noses to the ground, and worked our way down toward the creek bottom.

I could hear Plato talking as he sniffed for scent. "There's quail. There's rabbit. Cow. Raccoon. How about it, Hank, are you coming up with anything? Hank, I must tell you that my nose is very specific to quail, very specific, and I'm not sure that it will pick up a coyote."

"Quit yapping. That might help."

"Hank, I'm serious about this. I just don't think my equipment will work on coyotes, I really don't, so what I'm saying is that you might need to . . ." All at once he came to a dead stop. "Oh my gosh, Hank, here it is!"

I trotted over to him, put my nose to the ground, and checked it out. Sure enough, there it was: that peculiar, distinctively wild smell of a coyote. Just a whiff of it caused the hair on my back to stand up. It brought back many unpleasant memories.

I saw a look of pure terror in Plato's eyes. "What are we going to do, Hank?"

I swallowed hard. "We're going to follow it, what do you think?"

"Hank, I can't do this! I'm a bird dog and coyotes

just . . . I don't have any experience with . . . listen, Hank, coyotes scare me to death and I just can't handle this!"

I studied his face for a long time. Here was a guy I had disliked for years. I had always thought of him as a nuisance and a pest. He had stolen my girlfriend away from me. Now, I had the opportunity to laugh in his face and call him a coward.

But I didn't.

"Plato, let me tell you something. I'm just as scared of coyotes as you are. Being scared of coyotes is no disgrace."

His eyes turned into perfect circles. "Hank, no! I thought you said . . ."

"Never mind what I said. Here's the deal. Beulah needs our help."

"Hank, I know she does, but I just can't . . ."

"Hush. Your nose is about five times better than mine. We need your nose to find her. You find her and leave the coyote work to me."

He stared at me for a long time. "I thought you said you were scared of coyotes."

"I am. Any dog with a lick of sense ought to be scared of those guys. But sometimes we have to put duty ahead of our fears. And even our ambitions."

He took a deep breath. "You're right, Hank. I'm sorry I fell apart. I'll give it my best shot."

"That's all any of us can do, pardner."

He started away from me but stopped. "Oh, and thanks for what you said about my nose. I know that being a bird dog isn't all that great, but I'm proud of what I do."

"You've got a great nose, Plato. I watched you. You're a heck of a fine quail dog."

He beamed with pride. "Thanks, Hank. Thanks a whole bunch. I'll try to do my part."

"You'll do fine. Let's go find Beulah."

Our little conversation seemed to have brought him new reserves of courage. Too bad it didn't help me. My legs were shaking so badly that I thought I might fall over at any moment. Fortunately, Plato didn't notice.

He went charging into the tall grass and brush along the creek—nose to the ground and tail sticking straight out. He was a study in total concentration. His entire body seemed to be taking orders from his nose.

Me? To tell you the truth, I couldn't smell much of anything except ragweed, so it was a good thing we had Plato and his world-class nose out front and working the trail.

He really did have a great nose, and you know

what? Admitting it didn't hurt as much as I'd thought.

I could see that Plato was locked onto the trail of something. His body was bunched up and he had slowed to stealthy walk. Every part of him had shifted into slow motion except his nose, and it was out front, low to the ground, and working like a vacuum sweeper.

"What do you say, Plato?"

"Hank, I think we're getting close to something. I'm getting a strong reading on coyote, real strong. How about you?"

"Uh, the same, Plato, you bet."

"Say, those guys really smell bad, don't they?"

"If you think they smell bad, wait until you see their manners."

He gave a nervous laugh, then . . . he froze. "Hank, I think this is it. In those bushes, straight ahead."

A shiver of dread went through my body, but before I could think about it, I trotted past him and took over the Forward Position.

"Nice work, pal. I guess it's time for the Marines to take over. We'll see you after playtime."

"Good luck, Hank."

I moved toward the clump of bushes. My teeth were chattering so badly, I had to clamp my jaws shut. Five feet. Four feet. Three feet. Two, one.

I could smell him now, that wild musky smell that struck terror in the heart of a dog. I parted the bushes with my nose and . . .

There he was.

Will This Story End Happily or in Tragedy?

I would have been pleased to find Rip and Snort in the bushes. After all, we had been buddies on a few occasions and had shared some good laughs.

It wasn't Rip and Snort. It was Scraunch the Terrible, who happened to be the very worst, meanest, cruelest coyote in all of Ochiltree County. Or Roberts County. Or Lipscomb, Hemphill, Hansford, or any other county you could mention.

He was standing over Miss Beulah, holding her down with one huge paw.

I almost fainted when I saw his gleaming yellow eyes and scarred-up face. I was sorry that my sudden appearance didn't seem to have the same

effect on him. In fact, it just increased the size of his grin.

It took me a moment to find my voice. "Well, Scraunch, by George. Isn't this a coincidence, running into you out here in the, uh, bushes." He didn't speak, just glared. "And you seem to be standing on a friend of mine."

When she heard my voice, Beulah struggled to get up. "Oh Hank, thank goodness you found me! This horrible brute jumped me while I was getting a drink, and I think he's planning to take me as a captive. Get off of me, you big oaf, you're hurting my ribs!"

Scraunch got a chuckle out of that. "Huh, huh, huh. Horrible brute catch silly girl-dog away from house and boom-boom, now make her into coyote-girl to howl at moon."

She struggled again. "Oh no you won't, mister. I'll never be your coyote-girl, and furthermore, Hank is Head of Ranch Security and he beats up coyotes all the time, don't you, Hank?"

There was a long moment of silence. "Well, I, uh . . ."

"And he's going to beat you up SO BAD, you'll wish you'd kept your slimy paws to yourself, aren't you, Hank?"

"Well, I . . ."

"And then he's going to beat up all your cousins and uncles and brothers, aren't you, Hank?"

"Beulah, just lie still and let me do the talking. Please." She lay still, thank goodness, I mean, she was fixing to talk me into a shallow grave. She lay still and I turned to Scraunch.

He was grinning. "Dummy ranch dog beat up coyote all time, huh?"

"Well, she exaggerates, Scraunch, you know how it is."

"And beat up Scraunch and all kinfolks too, huh?"

"Well, maybe not all of them, but . . . listen, Scraunch, I'll bet we can work out a deal here. Let me have Beulah and I'll give you . . . let's see. I'll give you a free pass on my ranch. You can come and go as you please, do anything you wish. What a deal, huh?"

"Already got free pass." He held up a huge fist.

"Hm, good point. Okay, try this. Dinner for two at the chicken house. Absolutely free. All you can eat." He shook his head. "Okay, maybe you'd go for dog food, genuine Co-op dog food kernels. Great stuff, Scraunch, you'd love it." He shook his head. "Bones? We've got some wonderful bones."

"Ha. Coyote got plenty bones."

"Yeah, but these have been buried for months, Scraunch, my own personal collection of aged bones. I wouldn't offer this deal to anyone but you, no kidding."

He shook his head.

I was running out of ideas. I cocked my right ear, hoping to hear the sounds of the men coming in our direction. Where had they gone? If they didn't show up pretty soon . . .

I turned back to Scraunch. "Okay, Scraunch, I'll play my last card. Let Beulah go and take me as your captive. Make me your slave, eat me for supper, do as you wish, but let the girl go."

He gave that one some thought. "Pretty good deal . . . but not goodest enough. Hunk-dog too skinny for eat, too lazy for work, too ugly for look-at."

"Is that your last word?"

"Last word. Coyote tired of too much foolish talk." He beamed an evil eye at me. "Hunk-dog better git-go while gitting-go still good."

"All right, Scraunch, okay, you win."

"Huh. Coyote always win."

"I know, but before you carry this lovely lady off into captivity . . ."

Beulah let out a gasp. "Oh Hank, no!"

". . . before you carry her away, Scraunch, I want to sing her one last love song, just for old time's sake."

His face showed dill pickles and lemons—a sour expression, in other words. "Uh! Scraunch not give a hoot for dummy love song."

"That's fine, Scraunch, it's not for you anyway. You don't even have to listen."

He reached out a paw and poked me in the chest. "Hunk not tell Scraunch what to doing."

"Okay, fine. Listen to the song. It might improve your mind and upgrade your cultural standards."

He gave me a big wicked grin. "Scraunch not listen to dummy love song."

"That'll work. All right, Beulah, here we go."

"Oh Hank, don't abandon me to the coyotes!"

"Just listen to the song, dear. I think you'll find it pretty interesting."

Whilst I tuned up my tonsils, Scraunch turned his back on me and covered his ears with his paws while keeping a foot on Beulah. As you will soon see, he was walking right into my trap.

My Best for You

Beulah, collie of my dreams
With flaxen hair and eyes that beam
A light that warms me like the morning sun.
You do not know, I should not say,
I think of you most every day,
And dream of you when every day is done.

But there's a shadow in my dream,
A certain bird dog, and it seems
That you find him hard to ignore.
He's not a bad guy, I'll admit,
He's good with quail but I submit
That life with him could sure be a bore.

Now, Beulah, listen carefully,
There's more here than the eye can see,
This song is actually a secret code.
So do the things I say, my dear,
I'm going to bust you out of here,
And when I move you'd better hit the road.

When the music stops, I'll punch the brute
And do my best to break his snoot
While you and Plato run off to the west.
So don't look back but now and then
Remember that you had a friend
Who cared for you and gave you his best.

Scraunch missed the hidden message in the song, of course, but Beulah caught it. I could see the change in her eyes on the third verse. I gave her a nod of my head. She nodded back.

I took a big gulp of air and prepared myself for the next scene in My Life's Drama. "Hey Scraunch," I tapped him on the shoulder, "I'm finished." He turned around. "But I'm taking your nose with me. Here's a little bouquet from me and Beulah."

I drew back my right paw and delivered the hardest, straightest punch I could muster. I leaned into it, fellers, and gave it everything I had.

Ker-WHOP!

Holy smokes, that guy had the hardest nose in all of Texas! It was like slugging an anvil, a tree, a tombstone, a huge rock. It sent an earthquake through my paw, up my arm, through my entire body, and out to the tip end of my tail.

But you know what else? It knocked him backward one step, and that's all Beulah needed. In a flash, she scrambled to her feet and went streaking off to the west. On the other side of the bushes, she met up with Plato, and together they set sail for the house.

"Good-bye, Beulah," I heard myself say. "I wish it could have worked out better for us but . . ."

I turned my gaze back to . . . gulp . . . the horrible expression on his face sent shingles of sheer terror down my backbone, tingles, that is. Blood dripped off the end of his nose and there was a prairie fire raging in his eyes.

"Scraunch, I think I can explain everything if you'll just . . ."

"Ranch dog die!"

Before I could argue the point, or turn and run for my life, Scraunch leaped right into the middle of me and . . . that's all I remember.

He murdered me right there and that's the end of the story.

Sorry.

Okay, maybe he didn't quite get the job done, but only because the hunters came to my rescue and ran him off. He did pretty well, though, for a guy who'd been interrupted.

By the time the guys got there, Scraunch had shown me most of what he knew about boxing, pasture fighting, and Coyote Karate. He'd used my carcass for a basketball, a mop, a broom, and a dustpan, and then stuffed me into a hollow log.

That's where they found me. They saw my toenails sticking out of one end of the log. To get me out, they had to call in three winch trucks, two

units from the Wolf Creek Volunteer Fire Department, seven chain saws, and three welders with cutting torches.

Pretty serious, huh? You bet it was.

But then came the good part. They carried my near-lifeless body up to headquarters and laid me out under that big hackberry tree in the front yard—yes, in Sally May's precious yard.

Everyone was there. The whole ranch had turned out to see the Return of the Wounded Hero. Get this:

—The hunters raved about my bravery.

—Sally May fed me warm milk with a spoon and lavished her praise upon me for saving her, uh, turkeys.

—Plato said they should start a special fund at the First National Bank and erect a huge stone statue of me at the scene of the battle.

—Pete watched the whole ceremony from his spot in the iris patch. I had never seen him look so crushed. I loved it!

—And best of all, the lovely Miss Beulah hovered near my wounded side, called me her "extra-special friend" and even gave me a kiss on the cheek before she left.

Wow! Does it get any better than that? I don't think so.

Case cl . . .

Well, there was one small detail that bothered me. When Billy left our place around sundown, Plato and Beulah were standing in the back of his pickup.

Once again, the bird dog was leaving with MY GIRLFRIEND, which sort of made a guy wonder . . .

Oh well. In the Security Business, we take what's offered, and hope the rest will come down the road.

Case closed.

Have you read all of Hank's adventures?

1 *The Original Adventures of Hank the Cowdog*

2 *The Further Adventures of Hank the Cowdog*

3 *It's a Dog's Life*

4 *Murder in the Middle Pasture*

5 *Faded Love*

6 *Let Sleeping Dogs Lie*

7 *The Curse of the Incredible Priceless Corncob*

8 *The Case of the One-Eyed Killer Stud Horse*

9 *The Case of the Halloween Ghost*

10 *Every Dog Has His Day*

11 *Lost in the Dark Unchanted Forest*

12 *The Case of the Fiddle-Playing Fox*

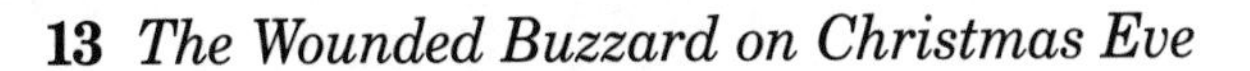

13 *The Wounded Buzzard on Christmas Eve*

14 *Hank the Cowdog and Monkey Business*

15 *The Case of the Missing Cat*

16 *Lost in the Blinded Blizzard*

17 *The Case of the Car-Barkaholic Dog*

18 *The Case of the Hooking Bull*

19 *The Case of the Midnight Rustler*

20 *The Phantom in the Mirror*

21 *The Case of the Vampire Cat*

22 *The Case of the Double Bumblebee Sting*

23 *Moonlight Madness*

24 *The Case of the Black-Hooded Hangmans*

25 *The Case of the Swirling Killer Tornado*

26 *The Case of the Kidnapped Collie*

27 *The Case of the Night-Stalking Bone Monster*

28 *The Mopwater Files*

29 *The Case of the Vampire Vacuum Sweeper*

30 *The Case of the Haystack Kitties*

31 *The Case of the Vanishing Fishhook*

32 *The Garbage Monster from Outer Space*

33 *The Case of the Measled Cowboy*

Join Hank the Cowdog's Security Force

Are you a big Hank the Cowdog fan? Then you'll want to join Hank's Security Force. Here is some of the neat stuff you will receive:

Welcome Package

- A Hank paperback embossed with Hank's top secret seal
- Free Hank bookmarks

Eight issues of *The Hank Times* with

- Stories about Hank and his friends
- Lots of great games and puzzles
- Special previews of future books
- Fun contests

More Security Force Benefits

- Special discounts on Hank books and audiotapes
- An original Hank poster (19" x 25") absolutely free
- Unlimited access to Hank's Security Force website at www.hankthecowdog.com

Total value of the Welcome Package and *The Hank Times* is $23.95. However, your two year membership is only **$8.95** plus $3.00 for shipping and handling.

To join Hank's Security Force, please send a check or money order for $11.95 ($8.95 plus $3.00 shipping and handling), payable to Maverick Books, to:

Hank's Security Force
Maverick Books
P.O. Box 549
Perryton, Texas 79070

Be sure to include your name, address, phone number, and your choice of a free book (choose from any book in the series). Please include two choices in case your first choice is out of stock.

DO NOT SEND CASH. NO CREDIT CARDS ACCEPTED.
Allow 4–6 weeks for delivery.

The Hank the Cowdog Security Force, the Welcome Package, and The Hank Times *are the sole responsibility of Maverick Books. They are not organized, sponsored, or endorsed by Penguin Putnam Inc., Puffin Books, Viking Children's Books, or their subsidiaries or affiliates.*

Visit the fan club website at www.hankthecowdog.com

John R. Erickson

began writing stories in 1967 while working full-time as a cowboy, farmhand, and ranch manager in Texas and Oklahoma—where two of the dogs were Hank and his sidekick Drover. Hank the Cowdog made his debut a long time ago in the pages of *The Cattleman*, a magazine about cattle for adults. Soon after, Erickson began receiving "Dear Hank" letters and realized that many of his eager fans were children.

The Hank the Cowdog series won Erickson a *Publishers Weekly* "Listen Up" Award for Best Humor in Audio. He also received an Audie from the Audio Publishers Association for Outstanding Children's Series.

The author of more than thirty-five books, Erickson lives with his wife, Kris, and their three children on a ranch near his boyhood home of Perryton, Texas.

Gerald L. Holmes

met John Erickson after moving to Perryton, Texas, a long time ago . . . and that's when Hank and his pals came to life for the first time in pictures. Mr. Holmes has illustrated numerous cartoons and textbooks in addition to the Hank the Cowdog series.